MRS. MO'S MONSTER

For Niamh

Thanks for the support & patience–
Mum, Mariesa, Doug, Bridge and Nicola

This edition first published in 2014 by Gecko Press
PO Box 9335, Marion Square, Wellington 6141, New Zealand
info@geckopress.com

Distributed in New Zealand by Random House NZ
Distributed in Australia by Scholastic Australia
Distributed in the United Kingdom by Bounce Sales & Marketing

First American edition published in 2014 by Gecko Press USA, an imprint of Gecko Press Ltd.
Distributed in the United States and Canada by
Lerner Publishing Group, Inc.
241 First Avenue North
Minneapolis, MN 55401 USA
www.lernerbooks.com
A catalog record for this book is available from the US Library of Congress.

DEC 0 3 2014

A catalogue record for this book is available from the National Library of New Zealand.

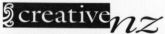

ARTS COUNCIL OF NEW ZEALAND TOI AOTEAROA

Gecko Press acknowledges the generous support of Creative New Zealand

Designed by Luke & Vida Kelly, New Zealand
Printed in China by Everbest Printing Co Ltd, an accredited ISO 14001 & FSC certified printer
ISBN hardback: 978-1-927271-00-1
ISBN paperback: 978-1-927271-01-8
ISBN ebook (EPUB): 978-1-927271-18-6
ISBN ebook (MOBI): 978-1-927271-26-1

For more curiously good books, visit www.geckopress.com
www.mrsmosmonster.com

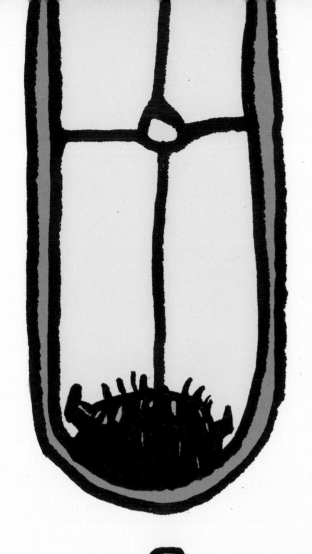

MRS. MO'S MONSTER

Paul Beavis

GECKO PRESS

One day

there was a knock at
the front door.

Mr. Mo was gardening,

so Mrs. Mo went to see who it might be…

TER.

He was looking for something to

CRUNCH, MUNCH, AND CHEW.

(That's what monsters do.)

"Not even a hello?" said Mrs. Mo.

"How rude."

Mrs. Mo soon found the monster crunching on a paintbrush.

"Excuse me,"
said Mrs. Mo.
"How will
we paint things
now?"

The monster thought and thought,
but he only knew what he knew,
so he roared, **"I CRUNCH, MUNCH, AND CHEW."**

And off he ran.

Next, Mrs. Mo found the monster munching on a ball of string.

"Excuse me,"
said Mrs. Mo.
"How will
we tie things
now?"

The monster thought and thought,
but still he only knew what he knew,
so he roared, **"I CRUNCH, MUNCH, AND CHEW."**

And off he ran.

A little later, Mrs. Mo found the monster chewing on a spoon.

"Now I know
what you *can* do,"
said Mrs. Mo.
"But shall we try
something new?"

"No!"

roared the monster.

"No, no, no."

And off he ran.

"That Mrs. Mo can't tell me what to do,"

he grumbled.

"I am a monster...

...and what I do is...

...CRUNCH

MUNC

and

When the monster had finished,
he wondered what else he could do.

He thought…and thought…

…and thought some more.

But still he knew only what he knew.

Then

he had an idea.

"Excuse me," said the monster. "What is this you do?"

"I'm painting letters," said Mrs. Mo. "Shall I show you how?"

"Hmmmm," said the monster.

"That's something I could never do."

"And what is this you do?" asked the monster.

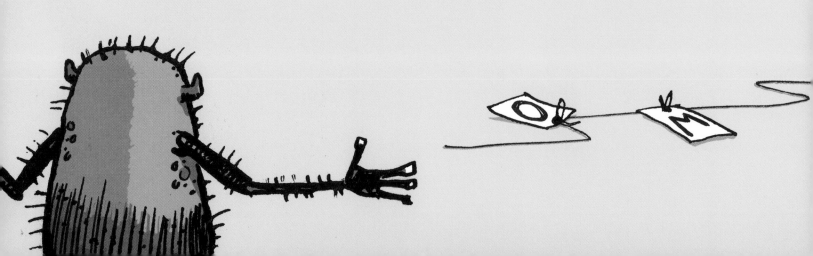

"I'm tying things,"
said Mrs. Mo.

"It's easy. You try."

"Ummmm," said the monster.
"That's another thing I could never do."

"Now what is this you do?" asked the monster.

"I'm stirring cake mix,"
said Mrs. Mo.

"Mmmmmm,"
said the monster.
"That's something…

And together they started to mix.

When everything was ready, Mrs. Mo and the monster shouted…

"Surprise!"

"Thanks ever so much," said Mrs. Mo.
"I couldn't have done this without you."

Just then there was

a knock knock

at the door.

Mrs. Mo and the monster

went to see who it might be…

...and in ran

TWO CHILDREN.

They were looking for something to

BASH, SMASH, AND THROW.

(That's what children do.)

"Not even a hello?" said the monster.

"How rude."